Moon Song

Stories

Moon Song

Stories

MaryAnn Williman

OCEAN PARK PRESS
Santa Monica, CA

For information contact:
Otto Williman
ottomatic59@gmail.com

ISBN 978-0-9899458-1-3

Ocean Park Press
Santa Monica, CA
info@oceanparkpress.com

MaryAnn Williman was a storyteller, and it started with her grandchildren. She would sit with them and weave wonderful stories. The characters were given the names of people she knew. Finally MaryAnn put the stories to paper and made up books for the grandkids. She was in the process of publishing these four stories in 2013 when she died. This book is lovingly dedicated to MaryAnn.

—OTTO WILLIMAN

"We are lonesome animals. We spend all of our life trying to be less lonesome. One of our ancient methods is to tell a story begging the listener to say, and to feel, 'Yes, that is the way it is, or at least that is the way I feel it.' You're not as alone as you thought."

—JOHN STEINBECK

Contents

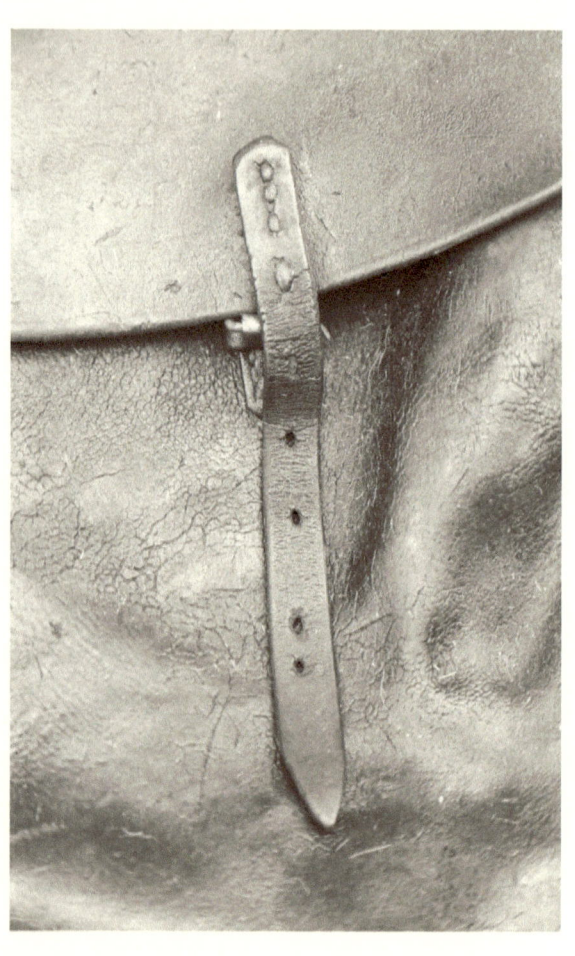

My Father's Purse

"HELEN, WHERE'S MY purse?" My dad would ask as he raced through the living room, frantically searching under magazines and newspapers.

"It's right where you left it dear." Mom would reply as she did every morning during "The Great Purse Hunt".

When I was much younger every weekday began with the family involved in "The Hunt". My two brothers had the job of looking in the high places. And since I was the baby, well, I looked low. Sometimes luck was with us and the missing purse was discovered within minutes but there were also those black mornings, when it eluded us as if it had a mind of its own.

However, I don't remember a day when it wasn't eventually discovered and then my Pop would open it and check the contents before stuffing it into his back pocket. A fast peck on my mother's cheek and a pat on the head of his children who stood, flushed and breathless and he was out the door.

I never realized then that most men didn't carry purses. So I guess my family was a little abnormal because none of us thought it was strange that the man of the house called his wallet, a purse.

And why would we? We were a family of readers that haunted the libraries and walked there every week and carried back the maximum number of books.

I loved the novels about Knights and Ladies. In those captivating tales, the jousts always had a "handsome purse". Robin Hood spent his days in the forest relieving merchants of their "fat purses".

Other books told of Prizefighters who fought for the title and "a big purse." Horse, boat, car, foot and yacht racing all had "cash purses". I devoured every word in those books and somehow "wallet" never found its way into any of the stories that lived between the covers of those tomes. A purse was exciting whereas a "wallet" was simply a piece of animal hide that encased money and identification cards.

So the fact that my father carried a purse was not odd to any of us living in that house. What was odd was the amount of things my father managed to carry in it. My father and his conjuror's bag showed me how to handle any emergency by simply being prepared and thoughtful.

His driver's license was paper clipped to his insurance card in the event of a moment's lapse in judgement. Written in his beautiful Philadelphia Lawyer's hand on the other side of that card, was my mother's name and number.

He carried no checkbook, credit or debit cards. No business cards or telephone numbers jotted down on torn off slips of paper. He had one picture of each of his 3 children, his favorite photo of us and I remember how stunned a lady at church was when she met my oldest brother home on leave in the 1950s. She had thought him to be a child of 12 or 13.

There was no health insurance card inside his purse. No pocket calendar or address book tucked neatly away in the corner. However, he did carry one check, one dime and a dollar bill. With those three items, my pop was prepared for anything.

With his dime, he could alert my mother as to the nature of the problem. With his dollar, he could buy a cup of coffee or cold root beer while he waited and with his blank check, he could pay for whatever had caused the difficulty.

I think often of my dad and his simplistic emergency system as I dig through my purse looking for my own checkbook. Digging through my "wallet" for one of five major credit cards and finally settling on a paperless check in frustration.

Periodically, my mother would update his unused check and void it. I never remember them arguing over the checking account as I sometimes do with my own husband.

"Where is check number 5456?" I demand.

"Look between 5455 and 5457?" He offers hopefully. And the battle is on again. How different it was when I was a child.

"Dan, here's a new check for your purse." My mother would say.

"Okay Pet."

"Don't forget to give me the old one."

"Just as soon as I find my purse." He would promise and my brothers and I would scatter before we were drafted into the Hunt again.

I remember how harmonious it all was. My mother ran the home and handled the finances. My father went to work everyday and carried a purse.

More Purse Contents

I LIVED IN that home for 20 years and in that time, my father pulled numerous valuable and imaginative things out of his purse. It was like a bottomless pit and could produce things on a moment's notice.

He always carried two Band-Aids and a foil-wrapped wound wipe. A paper clip, a rubber band and a postage stamp waited in some section of that incredible purse. I remember one time a stranger had locked his keys in his car and my dad and his straightened paper clip got that man home to his family.

The tiniest Swiss Army Knife rested comfortably somewhere in the confines of that purse and came to my own rescue one dark night many years ago.

The entire clan went camping during deer season and my Uncle managed to get one and bring it back to camp.

I learned that night about ticks. Once again, the contents of my father's purse did prodigious service. Those tiny tweezers inside that Swiss Army Knife coupled with a great deal of hollering produced a very chubby tick. A quick swipe with the wound wipe and I was on my way again, sorer but wiser.

"Walter's broken his shoelace Dear. Can you help?" My mother once asked.

"Let me look, Pet."

Now they didn't match in either length or color, but my cousin Walter got to finish playing in the family football game.

"Your daughter wants to go fishing, what have you got?" And my father produced a large safety pin and some string from some secret place inside his purse.

The fish I caught that day tasted flakier than anything I have ever landed on a chartered fishing trip. When I was young, all I needed was my father's purse.

"My head is killing me. I guess I'd better go home and take something." Mother said at one of our reunions and instantly two aspirins found their way into my father's hand. They weren't fancy ones with names like Bayer and Anacin. They probably upset your stomach if you took too many but they had the miracle ingredient that is in aspirin and the headache disappeared all because my father carried a purse.

The Fairy Tale Purse

WHEN I WAS 6 or there about (I know I was small enough for my dad to carry on his shoulders) somehow we ended up at an auction. In those days nobody had any money. Gas was less than 11 cents a gallon and we couldn't afford a car to put it in anyway. We rode with my beloved Uncle Fred, who had a station wagon that went down the road sideways because the springs were broken. He had so many kids himself that he said he never even knew that our family was with them.

People were bidding on things sight unseen and perched on my dad's shoulders, I had a ringside seat.

The Auctioneer looked right at my dad and said, "Who wants to bid on an empty box for a little girl?"

My dad yelled, "25 cents."

The Auctioneer barked, "SOLD, to the father with the little girl on his shoulders!" My dad walked to the front of the room, up to the table where they took your money. I was scared, I knew we didn't have any money and my dad would be embarrassed in front of all those people.

My father put me down and pulled his purse out of his back pocket. He winked at me and opened it slowly and began to thumb through it. I held my breath, I knew any minute he would have to tell the man that he had made a mistake and didn't have the quarter for the box.

That was the first time I ever experienced the magic of my father's purse. From somewhere in its dark recesses, just like Harry Houdini, he produced a quarter. He slid it across the desk and the man placed the empty box in my hands. We sat on some hay bales outside the auction tent and my father told me to open it.

Inside was Cinderella's glass slipper and sitting on a blue satin cushion in that slipper was a pretty wristwatch with a blue band. Cinderella danced with her Prince on the face while the hands ticked away the hours. Of course, the glass slipper was really plastic and the blue satin pillow was only a cotton ball covered with slippery fabric but I was enchanted nonetheless.

"Do you like it, Princess?"

Transfixed, I could only nod.

"Let's go find your mother and show her," he said getting up and dusting off the seat of his threadbare trousers.

I loved that watch the way one can only appreciate something that comes to them through magic. I wore Cinderella on my arm until the band simply gave out from use. I put her in my treasure box and kept her until I was a worldly-wise teenager of 17, and then I gave it to the Good Will. Two days later, I knew I had made a mistake. Things made of magic must never leave your side once they have found their way to you. My father's purse had brought it about for me and when I gave it away, some of my own magic went with it.

There's very little I wouldn't do to have it back in my life and yet I realize on some level that it belongs in the past. Back with the memories of my father and his magical purse, protecting my youth and wonder.

Where that quarter came from I do not know. We had no money for anything other than the necessities. A quarter bought a dozen eggs then or a quart of milk and a loaf of bread.

Once it even saved my father's life and if the magic was strong enough to do that, why do I still plague myself wondering about something as simple as a 25-cent piece?

The Strongest of Magic

MY FAMILY OWNED a Drug Store in the days before something called The Great Depression. My Grandfather was the Pharmacist and my dad worked the ice cream counter. His job included cleaning and restocking and general grunt labor.

My father would arrive after school and donning an apron and a silly looking paper hat would create tasty treats for his fellow classmates and the local customers waiting for their prescriptions.

At five o'clock, my Grandfather would hang

up the closed sign and walk home as he did every night. He ate at six every night, no matter what was going on in the world.

As soon as he left, my young dad would turn the radio up loud, and sing at the top of his lungs as he mopped or stocked the shelves. Sometimes a friend would drop by and my dad would sneak him in and they would sit at the counter and listen to a ball game.

But on this particular night, no friend had looked in and my father worked alone in the Store. The radio was broadcasting some very black news indeed. My dad was catching bits of it as he moved between the stock room and the ice cream counter. It was something about a big dip in the Stock Market. It was dire predictions for many people in business and he wondered a little if that would affect his dad.

He kept trying to change the station but they all carried the same unsettling news. At eight o'clock, he finished for the day and turned off the lights and stepped through the front door. Feeling in his back pocket and realizing he had forgotten his purse under the counter, he stepped inside to retrieve it, felt a rush of air and then a sound that he would remember for the rest of his life.

It seems there was a man who had his business office three flights up from the Drug Store. He too had been listening to the radio and the distressing news. He had just discovered that he was in financial ruin due to the crash of Black Tuesday. Not only was he now broke, he owed his creditors more money than he could earn in four lifetimes.

They think he must have sat all day, listening to the terrible news, praying for a miracle to save him but it didn't come and in his despair he wrote a note to his wife and children, opened his office window and leaped, head long through it.

In his panic, he never thought what would happen if someone had been on the sidewalk below. My father had been standing there an instant before but because of his magical purse, he had stepped back inside at the same instant the businessman fell to his death.

My father always said that his purse saved his life that day. Decades later he would tell the story and an involuntary shiver would pass over his body. When people asked for details, he'd shake his head and grow quiet.

Mary Sullivan's Beads

"'TWAS GREEN THEY were, you know. They'd have to be considering they had belonged to Mary Sullivan who was as Irish as Paddy's proverbial Pig. She was my father's mother, the Grandmother I never met even though I touched her Rosary Beads every week of my life when I was small.

My father was 16 and working after school in the Drug Store. His mother had been ill but the Doctor assured them that it was nothing serious. At three o'clock that afternoon, a neighbor lad stuck his head in the front door of the Drug Store and yelled, "Hey Moss! Your mom just died." Locking the doors, he raced home to see the Undertaker, leading two policemen, as they carried his mother's blanket-wrapped body on a stretcher.

He entered the house to find his family in various stages of grief and shock, covering the family pictures with dark cloths and stopping the clocks. He crept into the parlor where he had last seen his mother alive and ran his hands over the pillow where her head had rested. Sitting on the sofa, he pulled the pillow over his face and sobbed. When he had cried himself out, numbly he began to look around, trying to remember how she looked when he said goodbye that morning. His eyes fell on something that had fallen between the sofa cushions and reaching in, his hand came away with her Rosary Beads.

He remembered her telling him that she had won them in a Spelling Bee when she was a young girl. She had been school champion for her grade level and the Bishop himself had placed them in her hands. She treasured them above everything but her family. She had used them so faithfully over the years, that some of the beads had actually cracked.

They were all he had left of her and he carried them safely tucked away in his purse the rest of his life. He pulled them out every Tuesday evening when we went to church to say the Rosary. When one of our many relatives stepped from this world to the next, he'd take out his purse and out would come those green beads. I would watch my father's fingers as they slid across those small pieces of green glass, his lips moving in prayer. I always wondered if he felt closer to his mother at those times?

When I was 7 and made my First Holy Communion, the Nuns presented me with a child's size rosary. It was white and came in a little bag and I wore them, draped over my hands that day because the Nuns made me, but I never used them again. They disappeared as all things do we give no value to. Like my father, I used my grandmother's beads when it came time for any powerful praying. Somehow, when my fingers walked around those beads, the face of the grandmother I had never seen superimposed itself in my mind on what I believed God looked like. I prayed to God, but my grandmother was the one who heard my prayer.

My father carried them in a tiny cloth bag in his purse and when I would ask for them, he would open it and slide the Rosary into my hands. I knew that the green stones had to be emeralds because my father told me how priceless they were. I knew that anything I prayed when I held it was instantly granted.

Sometimes, growing up takes so much away from us. Those emeralds became cheap pieces of glass. I threw God away and my unknown Grandmother, stepped behind Him into the shadows. I grew up and married and went away and it was almost 20 years more before I found the face of God again. And when I did, I noticed that my pop had never stopped carrying Mary Sullivan's Beads in his purse.

My father lived to be almost 90. My brother, Danny took care of him for years before we finally had to give Pop up to the tender mercies of the AMA. He spent the last three years of his life in a Nursing Home.

Just before he died, he told my brother,

"You know, I'd like to see Montana."

"Montana?" my brother asked incredulously. "Why? Montana, we don't know anybody there."

"Well, I don't know but, I've never seen the Big Sky Country."

We thought no more of it because my dad was always planning to break out. He finally did escape. He slipped away very quietly one morning. The Nurses checked on him and his old worn out body was still lying in the hospital bed but his soul was on the highway back to God and I hope that his spirit was taking in the sights of Montana as he journeyed along.

We buried him in his suit that was much too big for him now. We placed Mary Sullivan's Beads in his hands so she would recognize him as he came through Heavens doors.

We placed his purse in his back pocket. Complete with postage stamp and Swiss Army Knife, two aspirins and all the rest of his emergency tools. We gave him a fresh dollar bill and a quarter because the price of a phone call has gone up. He has a new check too and we hope he buys something in Paradise because we would love to balance that bank statement.

Moon Song

Prologue

WE LIVE IN a twilight world, the bowl above us barren and dark. My sisters and I use all our woodland lore and ancient spells to keep the flora growing to feed the few people who populate our time.

Our sister Sarah, the Goddess of Hours, calls us to gather at each full turning of the Water Wheel, our only manner of marking time. We dance naked in the Sacred Grove before the stone altar, our pounding feet calling up the wind.

We feel it arrive, tugging at our hair, its force becoming more insistent until we must link arms, forming a circle to stand upright against its onslaught. Swaying and chanting together, we wait, for the gale to carry the voice of the Prophecy to us.

Anorac, the Wind Goddess feels it first. The subtle change in fierceness, and then Ullac's keen animal senses pick up the new consciousness. The force begins to cry as it tears through the branches of the ancient oaks, and I wait for it to invade my body, for I am called Stelari, the Keeper of the Prophecy. My sisters gather closer to me, lending me their strength to withstand the impact that is soon to overtake me.

It is here. It fills my senses and I feel my consciousness forced from my body as the words of the Prophecy pour from my mouth.

"A son will be born to warm the planet, a Golden One who will be a light for this dark world. With the coming of the Promised One, the land will prosper and grow fertile. With the birth of this child, humanity will become strong and continue. Fear and lack will disappear. Love and compassion will prevail, but the time has yet to come."

The wind releases me and I fall, my body twitching and jerking as I struggle to fight my way back into it. My sisters wipe my face and comfort me as the wind sighs, dying away. I force myself to stand. We are all young as we step into the Sacred Oaks, each one finding her appointed place within the Holy Grove.

I reach out and touch my tree. My hand dissolves into the bark; my hair becomes the hanging moss, my eyes and mouth, the deep burls in the trunk. We sleep, my sister goddesses and I, hidden in our oaks, at one with them, until the next turning of the Water Wheel.

The Crone Speaks

I AM NO longer young. I am alone. Two centuries passed while we waited for the fulfilling of the Prophecy. My sisters grew weary and lost hope. And when hope is dead, faith soon follows. One by one, they spread their cloaks and became one with the sighing wind. But I am Stelari and I am the Goddess of the Prophecy and the peace of death is kept from me. I must see the Prophecy fulfilled or watch our world die.

It is upon us. I have waited for this birth since the season of Eternal Shadows. Even now the Golden One struggles to be free of his mother's womb.

I know that this birth I wait to witness is the one the ancient Prophecy predicts. The Midwives busy themselves around the bed.

"The wind grows stronger. Soon your son will come forth," I tell the parents as I fight against its fierce power.

Father Storm holds his wife, Mother Earth, and encourages her as she struggles to bring life from her straining body. I close my eyes and whisper a prayer to Myrah, The Mother of All, to ease her pain. The Goddess smiles for I hear the small cry of their child.

At last, I think, he is here. The Prophecy has been fulfilled. My work is done. I can join my sisters.

An instant later there is an astonished cry from the women gathered around the new mother. A second child is being born. I rush to her side in disbelief.

"Another boy, twins!" The father shouts.

"No!" I cry. "This cannot be. The Prophecy does not speak of twins."

I know what I must do and my hand goes to the dagger in my pocket. This second child cannot live and I must be the one to take his life. My hand trembles with the deed it must perform, and horrified, I fall to my knees beside the bed. I pray for my sister's forgiveness, but I cannot do it.

"The Prophecy has described them well. See how golden and fair they are," the father says proudly, as he watches the midwives wrap the twins in blankets of cobwebs and moss.

The wind begins to howl through the birthing cave as the babes are placed in the mother's arms.

"Name them!" She demands of me.

"What of the second boy? The Prophecy has no name for him."

"Myn," yells the father, "Myn, for my own sire."

"And the other?" I ask pulling the Sacred Naming Crystal from my cloak.

"As the Prophecy has commanded," replies Mother Earth, looking at Father Storm who nods in agreement.

"Then awaken the Naming Crystal," I call to the ever-rising wind, "and let the ceremony begin."

It tears at our clothes as it lifts the Crystal high above us and sets it spinning. Faster and faster it turns, awakening the fire inside. The wind increases its savage attack upon the stone as we huddle together against its force.

Raising my staff with both hands, I bring it down hard, splitting the Crystal apart and releasing a waterfall of rainbow hues around the newborns and their parents as the wind shrieks and howls through the cave.

Leaning heavily on my oaken staff, I speak to them. "Your son, golden and fair, shall be the light of this world. The ancient Prophecy names him Sol and we have waited in darkness for him since the remembrance of time. Take him from this place to fulfill his destiny. You name the other Myn and I have not been given sight to see his future, but I know it would have been better if this child had not lived."

The wind eases, and the Crystal, dark and whole once again, falls at my feet. Leaning over to retrieve it, I feel my great age as never before. I return the stone to my cloak and leave the joyous parents with their new sons. I step out into the blackness and make my way back to the Sacred Grove where the wind awaits me.

"I have fulfilled my duty in the creation of the Prophecy and been witness to the beginning of the New Forever. I am weary and wish to rest but I am frightened by what is now unleashed in our world. Wind, ease my pain and speak to me. Tell me that the Prophecy speaks true."

"Rage and anger are born this night. Jealousy and spite are awakened by this birth. The Prophecy has been lost forever," it wails in my ears.

I shudder and cover my face with my hands

asking the Divine Forces to end my existence that I might not have to see the horror that is to come. Sobbing, I spread my arms

Father Storm's Story

TIME PASSED SLOWLY in our shadowy world and our twins grew steadily. But even we, doting parents that we were, began to see the ugliness that took root in our golden sons who vied for their mother's kisses and fought for my attention.

"Why must you always tear at each other so?" Mother asked them after one more, ugly scene.

Sol and Myn dropped their heads in shame, but the friction between them only grew deeper and the more they were punished for their behavior, the stronger their hate became until it took over all of our lives.

"You are two halves of the same whole and yet you argue and fight like sworn enemies." I reasoned with Sol, trying to understand what it was that drove him to this great distrust of his own image.

"Why must I share my world with a twin? I am the heir. I am the eldest son, the one that was prophesied! Myn would have it otherwise and I must always be on guard against him or he will take my rightful place."

I took Myn to the Sacred Oak Grove, foolishly thinking that he would be healed of his hate by the calm in that quiet place. But Myn simply said, "Sol thinks he is better because he is older. I should have been born first. He tells me that I will have nothing, that he will have it all and that I must come to him for the very food in my mouth. Never! How I hate him."

One night, sitting before the fire in our home in the Whispering Woods, I could be silent no longer.

"Our golden sons have brought discord and suspicion wherever they walk. I thought they might outgrow this spite but it only seems to have festered deeper. Their arguments are fierce and their boyish fights are now dangerous battles. Sadly, their hate has begun to affect the others that live here in peace with us. I am told the animals suspect the fish of plotting against them and that flowers now rage against the rain."

"Our world is in agony and it is all because of our boys," Mother sobbed. "I don't know what else to do."

"I have tried everything and they do not change. Their hate is a terrible living thing and if I do not act soon our world will never recover from this sickness that lives inside them," I told their mother, not looking at her for I knew what had to be done if our world was to be saved.

"But not yet my love, I could not bear it if they were banished."

"As you command me, my dear," I replied gratefully that the moment had not yet come.

• • •

But word soon came to me that Sol and Myn always competing undertook to test their strength, throwing rocks and then boulders and finally mountaintops. People lost their homes as these great missiles descended on them. Many animals were killed and rivers and streams became so clogged with stones that they could not flow to the sea. One night, an angry group of the world's citizens came to us, demanding something be done with the twins.

"What would you have me do?" I begged the leader.

"Come with us to the Sacred Grove and call upon the Crone and her powers to stop your boys," he replied and the others picked up the chant and I knew that the time I had dreaded had finally come.

We walked with torches and lanterns. All the people of our world united against my sons. I held my wife's hand and we wept as we walked and I thought how silent we were for such a great multitude. How would the Crone know we were coming? But then I felt the wind stir and moan, and I knew that she would be waiting, and my last hope for saving my sons died away on that same sobbing wind.

The Crone Continues

THE INSISTENT WIND calls me from my sleeping place inside the Vastness.

"Hurry," it wails. "The Prophecy is upon us."

I spread my arms feeling it blow through my soul as it carries me to the Sacred Grove. The light, cast by their torches, brings their shadows into the grove long before they arrive. I can see in the eerie light that they are being led by the Golden One's parents, and I wonder how these two grieving people can be the same happy couple who were with me in the birthing cave so many years ago. Silently, they form a circle around me and shove their spokesman before me.

"We have come," he begins fearfully, but I do not let him finish.

"Silence! Do you think I would not know why you disturb my slumber? Do you forget that the wind is both my eyes and ears while I sleep? I can taste your fear and the wind trembles with your anger. What would you have me do?" I ask the parents of the doomed twins.

"Our sons shared their birth, but they refuse to share our world. We come to beg you do what must be done," the father says, weeping.

"Do you understand that what I do cannot be undone?"

Father Storm nods mutely as his wife falls against him in her grief.

"Do you all ask this of me?" I yell at the mob and hear their condemning cries.

I raise my arms and call upon thunder and lightening to join us in the Grove, and rain, as always, followed.

"The two pieces can never be one but perhaps the two can work for the good of all. The Prophecy must come to pass or we are doomed to everlasting darkness. I command you all to stand with me as I pass judgment on them."

I send the wind to find the boys and bring them to us, and we wait, huddling against the driving rain. But only I know what a terrible judgment awaits them. Soon the angry wind returns, blowing the twins before it, into the grove where they fall on their knees before me.

"What is it old woman?" Sol asks arrogantly, as he stands, brushing leaves from his hair.

"How dare you bring us here," Myn barks as he rises, wiping mud from his beautiful golden face.

When no one speaks, the boys look at their parents and see them overcome with sorrow. As the angry mob closes in, I can sense the fear that is beginning to grow in the brothers.

Sadly I lift my staff and speak. "Unhappiness and strife came into our world with your first cries and it grows weary under your malice and hate. The people cry because of your actions just as the rain, now falling upon you, weeps. I raise my hand and point at Sol.

"From this moment forward you will be known as Sun. You are banished to the heavens above our world where your golden light will bring day into being."

Thunder follows my words and Sun falls to his knees in terror. I turn to his brother and shout above the wind. "I, Stelari, separate you forever. You Myn, are now Moon and your golden light

I send to the bottom of the sea where you will guide fishermen in their ships by night. You will ever be apart, Sun leaving his bloody fingerprints in the sky as night approaches, and Moon's light swallowed by the waves each dawn."

As my words die away, lightening strikes somewhere in the grove causing the ground to tremble, and Moon screams. The mob takes up stones and chases the brothers out into the dark, as Sun turns eastward to take his place in the sky where he will know loneliness. Moon walks west and into the ocean depths to be abandoned by all.

Moon's Tale

MY BROTHER AND I now mark the passage of time for our world, but for myself living under the sea, time has no beginning or end, for loneliness is eternal. How many centuries I have lived thus, I cannot know, but on this infinite night, I am aware of a new sound from the sea. Hauntingly and low it flows over the water to my straining ears.

"What can it be, after all these years alone here?" I ask the waves.

"We have birthed a new species called Lorelei. Her language is the siren's song and the earth people have named it Mermaid."

"I must see this creature for myself. Take me to where it feeds," I command.

The waves then swelled and carried me away to the Sighing Caverns and there sitting among the rocks sat the Lorelei. As I crept closer, enchanted by the sound it made, it saw my golden light and dove deep into my waiting arms.

"What manner of beast is this that has such a sorrowful voice and yet radiant eyes?" I ask the silent sea.

Every night after that I came to the rocky place to hear the Lorelei's voice, and with each note the creature melted all feelings save love in me. I knew that I will worship the Mermaid until the Mystical Every Where exists no more.

My brother separates us each dawn and I return to the bottom of the sea and envy him his time with her. Each time Sun leaves the world,

I leave the ocean depths in darkness and go and find my love.

One night as I was leaving, the waves warned me, "Your great light is missed upon the sea. Sailors cannot find their way and ships have sunk and many lives have been lost while you wait upon the Mermaid and lose your strength."

I too, had heard the sailor's cries, but my love for the Lorelei was greater than my duty. The Crone sent the wind to speak to me, but my lovesick ears heard only the Mermaid's song. My light was only for her now and as my love deepened, my will and golden strength disappeared.

Brother Sun's Story

THE CRONE'S WIND tears at me and gives me no peace whispering tales about my hated brother's new love. It taunts me because I am not the one she favors, tempting me to act while Moon grew weak.

"Your brother has something more than you will ever know. Will you not take this thing from him while his energy ebbs, or will you allow him to keep it and be greater than you at last?"

Upon hearing this, I grow angry and go in search of my brother's creature. I find her using my golden light to warm her self while she rests upon the rocks. How lovely it is, I think and know then that I want her for my own. Somehow, I must take her from my brother and this I plot against Moon's happiness.

I begin to woo her by sending gentle showers to wash her silvery hair, but she turns her back to me. I then cause the flowers to grow during their sleep time, yet it means nothing to the Mermaid. I send my golden rays to kiss her face but she only laughs at me.

"Will you not look upon me with love?" I ask, but she dove deep into the sea to be nearer my brother. My twin's hate had never beaten me, but his love has finally won and I vow vengeance.

"If you will not accept my love, than you will feel my rage," I roar, and my anger scorched the earth. As I storm against her, rivers and streams dry up and fires race through the Whispering Woods. My rage grows, making me stronger and destroying my mind until I am not capable of rational thought and in anger, I commit the unspeakable deed.

I rise at dawn and lay in wait for the Lorelei. When I hear her song dying away on the morning breeze, I reach out and rip her voice from her throat and throw it from me into the heavens. And, still raging, to my great shame, I pull the Mermaid from the water and tear her in two and send her after her song.

At last, my rage spent, I begin to see the horror of my actions and I scream, "Wind, blow me far away that I do not have to see what I have done this day."

But the wind only beats against my broken heart and carries my mournful wails over the sea, and, in my shame, I turn and hide in the shadow of our world, leaving the land below in darkness during my time in the heavens while I cower here.

Moon's Song

I AWAKE TO silence. The wind does not carry my beloved's voice to me even when I command it. Night after night I search straining to hear her, but only stillness greets me.

"Where is she?" I ask the waves, but they remain silent.

Frantic, I search, screaming out her name and as time passes with no answer, I begin to go mad. Months go by before I am able to accept that she was gone from me. I then return to the deepest part of the sea and mourn for her.

"You must stop crying," the waves beg me.

"I am lost and I cannot live without her. My life has no meaning now that her song is gone."

"You have dimmed your golden light with your tears. The waters have grown dark again," the sea wailed.

I knew then what my fate must be.

"Will you help me, old friend?" I ask the Deep and in reply it lifts me high in its watery arms and I begin my journey toward the land where the waves break against my spirit and cast me upon the shore to die.

There I struggle in the dark sea, the cruel wind carries my brother's voice to me, and I know that he has come to torment me in my dying.

"Brother, forgive me," he pleads, and even in my agony, I know that something is different between us. He lifts me from the waters and holds me in his golden arms.

"Brother, I have missed you. Forgive me for hating you," I whisper.

"I have wronged you and I await your punishment," he answers humbly.

"I think we have both been punished enough, brother."

We then sat and spoke quietly of our loss and loneliness, and peace came upon the land.

The Crone's Wind

THE WIND BEARS me to where they wait, the Golden Ones, once so alike and now forever different: Sun so strong and, Moon, now so desolate.

Laying my hands upon their heads, I say, "The Prophecy has truly been fulfilled, what was separate is now made whole. Brother has united with brother and balance has come to our world.

"At least, we shall be together in peace," Moon says looking at his brother. However, it is known that even this small thing will be denied them.

"Your love has healed the hate that once lived inside you but the Prophecy cannot be rewritten, Golden Sun is to guide the day and empty Moon to guard the night."

The brothers, accepting my words, hug one last time and Moon starts down to the dark sea below, but I stop him,

"The sea is no longer your home, you are to live above our world and share its heavens with your brother. The Prophecy commands that you follow one another through the skies but never meet again."

The wind pushes forlorn Moon to his place in the night sky where he sits dark and unseen by the people below. All his golden brilliance is lost in his grief for the Mermaid. Sun, seeing his brother so lost in the darkness, yells, "I shall leave some of my light in the heavens for you to use each night."

Sun, weeping, returns to his home high above our world. I whisper into the wind and send it forth to grieving Moon saying, "Tonight, new beings appear and the people shall call them stars. Your brother has created them to share the night with you. Listen well for they are the voice of the Lorelei. She lives in the constellations the stars create."

"I give you back your love, Moon. The Lorelei and her songs are yours for eternity. I thank you and your brother for the light you bring in to our world."

But Moon does not hear my word; he is already lost to his Lorelei.

"Come wind, I grow weary with this tale. The Vastness beckons to me and I am anxious to see my sisters again."

I spread my cloak and disappear on the night wind.

Through the Doggie Door

"MORGAN?"

The aging black and white Border collie slept with his head on his paws. He was dreaming again of corralling fractious sheep with the speed of his long-ago youth.

"Morgan? Come on Woofie, wake up," the insistent voice demanded.

Morgan whimpered and left the wonderful dream as he cocked his ears in the direction of the annoying voice.

"Ah, good. You're awake."

"Moss? Is that you, Moss? What's up? Why are you waking me? What time is it anyway?" Morgan asked sleepily.

"I'm not sure, but it's late. The Dog Star's been chasing its tail across the sky for hours. Are you good and awake now, Morg, because I've got to tell you something?" his brother Border collie asked.

"Give me a second, friend," Morgan replied as he pulled himself to his feet, stretched his rump high, then pushed his chest forward and straightened his back legs until he was standing on his toenails. He yawned noisily, then shivered the length of his body. He settled on his rump, ears, nose and failing eyes on his oldest companion.

"Morgan, I've got to go away and I wanted to say goodbye and let you know that you're in charge now," Moss began.

"What? You can't go anywhere. Why our humans aren't even up yet."

"Woofie, quit talking and listen to me. This isn't my choice but I have to leave."

"Well you just can't right now. Our mom has to have that awful surgery and she needs all of us around her, woofing her through it. So forget it, because you aren't going anywhere," Morgan stated firmly and turned his back on his brother.

"Morg, old pal. My time is up. I was only given so many tail wags. I've only a handful left, and I'm going to need them on the road home to the Alpha Dog's lair."

Morgan turned back, tears in his dimming eyes. For the first time he was grateful for the white film that was taking his vision because it wouldn't let Moss see him cry.

"How long have you known?" he managed to choke out.

"For at least seven supper bowls," Moss started. "I think I heard it first, a sighing wind moving through the long grasses, but when I looked, there wasn't even a breeze. I knew then that it was The Whistling Wind but I didn't want to believe it."

"You don't know that for certain. You know how tricky the wind can be," Morgan said, hopefully, placing a paw on his brother's shoulder, looking sadly into Moss's furry face.

"And for the last three nights, I've heard Megan baying in my dreams, inviting me to chase her."

Morgan dropped his head. He knew that his sister Megan had been gone from the family for three summers. She was the first of the pack to leave and he still felt sad when he remembered her scent.

"So brother Morgan," Moss said, interrupting his thoughts, "I'm very tired. It's my time and I need to go and fill my nose with new smells. To be honest, my old feet are itching to chase something exciting again. I'm gonna miss you and the young pups, but I'll miss Mom most of all," he said wistfully, looking toward her bedroom.

"But what about her operation? What will I tell her? She doesn't need this right now, you know."

"I know Woofie, but Mom's going to need

Megan and me pulling on her leash from upstairs. You and the pups will be here for warm snuggles when she needs them, but we need to be waiting on the other side of the door if she doesn't make it."

Morgan nuzzled his brother and breathed his scent deep into his nose. They sat, touching muzzles and listening to the silence. Mom coughed and Moss winced and pulled away.

He put his head down and came up with his ball in his mouth. He placed it in front of Morgan, saying, "There you go, old man. Keep track of it for me, will you?"

Morgan choked back tears as he asked, "When are you leaving?"

"Actually, I'm already gone. Just this worn out old body's left. I have to leave something for Mom to hug goodbye. I'm relying on you to let her know that I'm okay with going. Can you do that for me, Woofie?"

"You know you can," his littermate answered.

"All right then. Keep your nose into the wind

because you're the Top Dog around here now. See you, friend."

Moss turned and scooted through the doggie door. Morgan pushed his nose against the flap intending to follow but the further Moss got from the door, the lighter and faster he moved. Morgan's nose twitched twice when Megan appeared and bayed to her brother. Moss perked his ears at her call and raced off after her.

"Good Woofies," Morgan called softly after them.

"Woof, woof, wooofff!" he heard them respond.

Morgan watched them until they disappeared into the night, then he backed through the doggie door and found his favorite sleeping spot again. He rested his head on Moss's ball and waited for the coming of day.

• • •

"Come on, sweetheart, try to get up and come outside with us," his cousin Muse coaxed.

"Yeah, you can do it if you try hard," Moon and Mulph said in unison.

"I wish it was that easy," Morgan said groaning with his effort.

"Lean on us Woofie and we'll get you outside," Muse promised, and somehow, with the strength of the pack, Morgan found himself out in the morning light with the familiar damp grass under his paws. He threw back his graying head and pulled the scent of the day deep into his nose.

Ah, Dad's out here already and that means spring must be here, he thought, as he looked for his favorite spot to relieve himself. He could feel the young ones watching him and it made him grumpy and he growled at them.

"Doggone it! What's the matter with you? You act like you've never seen a dog lift his leg before. Quit being such old hens, and go and enjoy yourselves."

"Sorry old man," said Mulph. "Just trying to help out." And he bounded off with the others in close pursuit.

Morgan snuffled and made his slow way to the big oak tree. A long time ago, when he was just a pup, he had taken ownership of the giant. None of the others had ever questioned his right to it, not even his big brother Moss.

Those were good days, young and carefree, and all that energy to run and fetch. Where did it go?, he wondered as he settled down in the shade of the tree. Off across the meadow he could hear the pack bow-wowing and chasing after one another.

Morgan had to use his nose and ears to keep informed about what was going on in his domain now that he was almost completely blind. He could still see Mom though because she always had that golden light around her. He curled up and listened to the sounds of his world as it moved around him. Pretty soon the warmth of the sun and the sounds of the insects in the flowers lulled him sleep.

• • •

"Morgan! Hi ya Woofie. How's the kid?"

"What? Who's there?" Morgan woke with a start and stuck his black nose into the air trying to locate whoever it was that had spoken.

"We're waiting for you, old timer. Come and play fetch with us," the dream voice coaxed.

"Grrr! Who is it? Bark! Get over here where I can see you if you know what's good for you!" Morgan growled.

But, then he heard it: the wind moving through the long grass of the meadow, calling to him. Startled, he sat up like a young pup.

"You're getting it, Woofie!" The voice praised.

"Moss, is that you Moss?"

"None other," the voice replied.

Frightened, Morgan quickly understood his wags were running out, "How long do I have? Do you know? What if I don't have enough time to say goodbye?"

"You'll have all the time you need friend. Loving folks takes no time at all. It's the apologizing for not loving that steals all our life from us." Moss replied with a chuckle.

"I don't know if I'm ready yet? I don't even know if I want to go? How can I leave our humans? What about those young dogs there?" he asked angrily as he watched the pups wasting their precious wags chasing butterflies. "Do you think any of them is ready to be Top Dog?"

"Relax brother. The decision doesn't have to be made today. The Alpha Dog just put me on a long leash so I could come and break the news to you. Now put a smile on your kisser, because Mom's coming. Boy, she looks great, doesn't she? I've really missed her tummy rubs."

The two Border collies watched her walk toward them. She wore a wide brimmed hat over her riotous curls. A soft, trailing scarf warmed her neck and shoulders and she hummed one of her strange songs. She smiled when she saw Morgan.

"There you are. I've brought you a treat because you're such a good Woofie." She sat beside him and broke it in small pieces because his teeth were not what they once were.

"How curious," she said, looking around, "I could swear I heard Moss panting."

"It's nice to know that I haven't lost my place in her heart," Moss said, lovingly.

She sat down and began to sing one of her soft tunes while she scratched Morgan behind the ears. He sighed contentedly and put his head in her lap. Moss circled three times and lay down next to her. The old tree sheltered them, the two that still breathed the spring air and the ghost dog that inhaled celestial ethers. Thus they passed the long hours of "Dog Watch", together again, as the sun went down behind the barn.

. . .

"Woofie? Are you okay, Sweetie? Please open your eyes and let me know you're all right?"

Morgan could hear Mom's voice, but she

sounded so far away and he was going to have to lift his head, but he didn't have the energy.

I'll just give her a small wag or two, he thought.

"Oh Morgan, thank heavens you're alive," she cried when she saw the feeble movement of his tail.

Morgan didn't know why Mom was so upset. In fact he couldn't figure out much of anything. His body felt strange and heavy and yet his mind seemed to be wrapped in a soft blanket. He had the most marvelous sensation of floating out of his crippled dog form.

Now if Mom and Dad would just quit fussing over me, this would be a fine place to finish my journey, he thought.

"You relax, big guy," Dad said. "We've called the vet and he's waiting for you."

Oh good, Morgan thought, "I woof that new doctor. He has kind eyes and his paws are gentle." But then, Dad picked him up and the pain came. Morgan had to run away and hide from the terrible burning in his head. He wasn't even aware of being carried to the car.

• • •

"It's probably a stroke," the vet said. "He's 15 now and that's getting up there for his breed."

Morgan opened one blind eye and wondered which dog the vet was talking about.

Surely, it can't be me, he thought, I can't possibly be that old. Megan and Moss, now they were old dogs, but me, why I'm still full of wags. Then Morgan heard Mom and Dad crying and he knew, he knew!

"Here's some medicine to ease his pain and here's a prescription for an antibiotic that may or may not help. Only time will tell, and we'll hope for the best."

Dad picked Morgan up and the awful pain came and Morgan followed his nose far away.

• • •

"Woofie? Come on old pal, it's me, Moss. Time to go. The Alpha Dog's waiting for you."

Morgan fought his way up out of the darkness that engulfed him.

"Moss is here and is talking to me but why can't I see him?" he wondered.

"There you go. Push against the softness, and twitch your ears in my direction," Moss urged.

"Arf?" Morgan managed even though he was trying his doggondest to speak.

"Good man. You're almost there. A little further now. Great, you made it. You're back!"

"Was I gone somewhere?" Morgan asked, sitting up and trying to focus his attention on his litter mate.

"You really don't know what happened, do you?"

"No, did something happen I should know about?" Morgan asked with a yawn.

"Nothing too exciting, Kid. You had a stroke and dropped your body, but then you got scared and stepped back into it. Now you're kind of hanging between the two layers," Moss replied.

"Wow, I did all that? Why don't I remember any of it?"

"You're not supposed to, Woofie. Anyhow, that's not important, but this is. Are you ready to let it all go and come and join me and Megan?"

"Wait, wait, my brain hurts and I'm having a hard time thinking straight. Can I have a minute?"

"Sure, take all the time you need, but I want you to look over your shoulder and tell me what you see," Moss directed.

Morgan did and his breath whooshed out in a tiny "arf," realizing he was looking at his own aged body, wrapped in towels. He looked closer and saw his tongue hanging out and that he was drooling like a tiny puppy. He noticed how gray his once black hair was. Then the mirror he was looking into opened its eyes, and Morgan sensed there were no wags left in them. He watched his ears twitch feebly, and he knew that Moss was right; it was time to go.

He realized he was actually seeing for the first time in many years.

"Will my eyes stay like this?"

"Nope. They'll get even better the longer you're gone from your old skin. Everything gets sharper and stronger. It's like being born again or being born a new pup with a lifetime's experience inside yourself. It's pretty doggone wonderful, Kid."

"And Mom and Dad? Does this sadness at leaving them get any easier?" Morgan asked, looking down the hall at the room where they slept.

"I'm not gonna lie to you, chum. That's the only tough part about leaving, but they still have Moon and Muse and Mulph to help them get through your passing."

"Who will be the Top Dog now?"

"They'll have to work it out among themselves, I expect."

"Am I permitted to say goodbye?"

"Sure Woofie. I'll wait here."

Morgan stepped quietly through the dark house, tip-pawing around assorted yellow duckies, balls and socks, so stretched in tug-o-war that they'd never be worn again. He looked in at his three cousins where they slept, curled up together for warmth and comfort. He murmured a soft "Woof now," but only Muse stirred in the moonlight streaming through the window.

As quietly as a shadow, Morgan entered the den of his humans. Using his newfound vision he gazed a long while at his folks snuggled close in the big bed. Mom stirred and her hand dropped over the side close to his nose. Very gently, so as not to wake her, he sniffled and snuffled the scent of it to take away with him to remember when he lived among the stars. She must have sensed his presence.

"Morgan?" she murmured.

As quietly as he entered, he retreated. One final trip through each room and he was ready to go with his brother Moss.

"Leaving anything behind?" Moss asked as

Morgan continued to sniff at everything about him.

"No," he replied, "just want a nose full to remember on winter nights by the fire."

"Follow me then through the doggie door and stay close. Megan's waiting on the other side to guide us home."

Moss pushed the flap open with his head and Morgan scrambled through behind him.

"How far is it?" Morgan asked, puffing with the exertion.

"It's just a wonderful run away, and fetch never ends because nobody ever gets too tired to play," Moss promised.

As his brother had predicted, the more Morgan ran, the easier it was and the more he barked and grr'd, the younger he felt. He grinned and looked as far ahead as his new sight would let him and he saw his sister Megan waiting for them.

"Woof," he called.

"Woof, woof, Woofie," she answered.

Morgan felt the softness of the sky all around him. It called to him, and he had an overpowering urge to leap into it. His brother and sister were paw-steps ahead.

"Come on, Morgan," they barked.

Giving in to the feeling, Morgan leapt after them.

"Last one home, is a mangy cat," he barked back.

The three Border collies chased and raced each other through the starlit night.

The Becoming of Hiram

HE HAD NO idea where he was or how he came to be there. It was dark and cold but not uncomfortable. He knew he wasn't alone although he had neither eyes to see nor ears to hear. Feeling snug and safe, he waited.

In time, it grew warm and wet and felt so comforting that even though he had no mouth he smiled and settled in to wait a little longer.

Later, a curious sensation moved through him and he yearned to stretch, but was too afraid. He pushed the feeling away, choosing to wait some more.

The darkness softened to gray as light encroached. When it touched him, the urge to reach upward was very strong but fear still held

him, and he continued to wait, and wait and…
wait.

The light intensified, as did the feeling. At
last, yearning overcame his fear. With one huge
push, he left the familiar place and followed the
light as it drew him up and out, to lie gasping in
its warm caress.

Where am I? He wondered.

"Welcome, Hiram. We've been waiting for
you for a long time," a voice answered.

"Hiram? Did you call me Hiram?" "Who are
you and how do you know my name? Where am
I?"

"Whoa, one thing at a time," chuckled the
voice.

"We'll answer all your questions but now you
need rest from your long journey," a new, softer
voice added.

"Is this place very far from where I began?"
Hiram yawned.

"Oh yes," said the soft voice. "You're in a new
world now."

"I am tired but I'd like to know where I am before I sleep," he pleaded.

"Why Hiram, this is the Garden of Earthy Delights," the deeper voice replied.

Satisfied, he succumbed to a deep weariness. He nestled into a warm and cozy spot and slept.

"Is he awake yet? How much longer before he opens his eyes?"

Hiram became aware of voices speaking very close to where he rested. He yawned and stretched in the bright warmth and wondered why he'd been so afraid to come to this wonderful new place.

"Morning Hiram!" said one.

"About time you got up," said two.

"Hurry, we want to meet you!" said three.

"Open your eyes," begged four.

"My bothers are such pests. They're young and not grown up like me," said a fifth, feminine voice.

"Get a load of Miss Maturity!" Chimed the four voices as one.

"Hiram, these are my baby brothers, Ham, Lam, Ram and Sam and I'm Sylvia. We're five peas in a pod, we do everything together, like it or not."

"Don't listen to her. She thinks she's the boss of us because she's the girl," said Ham and Lam together.

"Miss "hoity-toity" thinks she's smarter," echoed Ram and Sam.

"Honestly, do you see what I have to put up with? No girl should have four brothers. I'm happy you're here. You can be my special friend."

Hiram felt shy and awkward listening to the five bickering peas. Goodness, he thought, how strange this place is! Then, the deep voice that had welcomed him yesterday spoke, "All right, little ones, settle down or our friend here will be sorry he made the journey."

Ham, Lam, Ram, Sam and Sylvia stopped talking. Five round, green faces peeked over the edge of their pod and smiled at Hiram.

"There, that's better isn't it? Allow me to

introduce myself. I'm Leroy, a member of the Eggplant family, the Purple Eggplants from Virginia," he said bowing low.

"Ahem," interrupted the soft voice.

"Excuse me, my dear. This lovely ear of corn is our Ginger," he continued."

"Pleased to meet you, Hiram," she said extending a leaf.

Hiram looked into her brown eyes and blushed. The Pea Pod kids giggled, making it worse.

"That's enough. Everybody get back to what they were doing while Ginger and I try to help Hiram find his roots," Leroy said as he shooed the Peas off.

"The first thing you need my friend is a cool drink. Are you thirsty from your long wait?" Ginger asked, showing Hiram a pool of water that encircled his roots. She scooped some up in her leaves, dipped her silky brown head and drank deeply. Still smiling, she offered it to him.

What extraordinary stuff it is, he thought

as the water raced through him and gave him energy. The last vestiges of sleep left and he smiled.

"That's the ticket. Now you're getting it," said Leroy beaming.

"What was that?" He asked.

"Water, dear. All vegetables need water to grow. Without it, we would wither and the wind would blow us away," she replied.

"Vegetables? What did you say?" He asked.

"Vegetables, Hiram. You, Leroy and the others here in the garden, we're all vegetables."

"And you, my confused friend, are a Pumpkin, a member of the Squash family. Your people have been in this country for generations, your roots go very deep," Leroy informed him.

"I think he's has had enough information for one day. He looks rather stunned." Ginger cautioned.

But then, a new being appeared in the garden and the other vegetables grew very excited. It was so big, and it moved! Hiram put his leaves over his face to keep from crying out. He heard the peas laughing and he was embarrassed again, but then the stranger stopped right in front of him.

"Well, look who's finally here. Welcome, little pumpkin, I've been waiting for you for a long time," the newcomer said as it touched him gently, pushing the leaves from his face.

Hiram loved the way it felt and his fear left. He wanted this new being to be with him always. When it moved away an aching loneliness filled him.

"What kind of vegetable was that?" he asked, when the being left and closed the gate.

"That wasn't a vegetable at all, son. That was a human from the Farmer family and he tends our garden and keeps us healthy as we grow here."

"I liked it when he touched me."

"Yes, Hiram, it feels that way to all of us. We're very connected to the farmer. We have a special bond that you'll learn about in time. It's called The Becoming," Ginger said.

"But for now, it's time to relax and grow. The sun is warm and the garden's very peaceful. Why don't we just enjoy it for awhile?" Leroy asked.

Hiram settled back with his new friends and began the process of Becoming.

He loved the garden and his life there. A feisty celery stalk named Josh was his best friend even though the turnips said that he'd probably come to a bad end. But even their dire predictions couldn't dim those warm golden days.

Each morning, the farmer came and walked among them. He uttered strange sounds that were very pleasing. Hiram asked Leroy how the farmer made the noise.

"Humans have mouths for singing. They have eyes and ears and noses too, and hearts that sometimes end up broken. They have a spoken language and a remembering mind."

"Sit back, Honey, it's time we told you of The Becoming," Ginger said as she joined them.

"Yes, we usually save this topic for long summer nights but there's no time like the present is there?"

Leroy began. "The only thing you need to know is that something called "The Source" lives in everything and everybody. It's as strong in you as it is in the human."

"Looks like it missed you though," Josh teased from his place in the garden.

"Quiet Josh! This is important for Hiram to learn," Leroy scolded. Shading his purple head with his leaves, he continued.

"Now where was I? Oh yes, The Source is in all of us, but, strangely, sometimes we feel we're all alone."

"Nobody feels lonely while I'm around," Josh yelled as he chased the green onion kids through the carrot patch.

"Ignore him Hiram," Ginger said giving Josh a look that would have wilted lettuce.

"So, we know about The Source but, because we're vegetables and can grow only in a garden, our thought of The Source is confined here too. By the end of summer, when all of us have left here, we take our knowing about The Source with us and the garden lies fallow until the new vegetables are planted in the spring," Leroy said.

"But the new vegetables must feel The Source while they're sleeping don't they?" Hiram asked. "I felt something while I waited."

"Yes, because we leave our echoes behind for them," said Ginger with a small smile.

"Quite right, my dear, but sometimes even vegetables become rootless. Maybe there's so much rain that the seeds are washed away. Or perhaps there's too little and nothing grows. Those are sad times and our echoes of The Source are not enough. That is when we must rely upon the humans to remember for us," Leroy added.

"Oh," said Hiram. "You're talking about their remembering mind."

"Yes, but also about our part in The Becoming. Humans have no roots to hold them down. As they go from place to place, they use their language to talk about The Source. If the humans had no food to sustain them, they would die and The Source thought would be lost to them forever. Our purpose is to grow and be nourishing food so they can hold The Source thought in their minds. Do you begin to understand, Hiram?"

"I think so."

"Good, then that's enough for today. Why don't you go play with Josh and the pea pod kids," Ginger coaxed.

Hiram found them kicking dirt at a group of grumpy tomatoes and he soon forgot about everything and joined them.

"What is it?" Hiram asked as the sky lit up and the garden shook with explosive sounds.

"I don't know, but isn't it great?" Josh smiled as he craned his long neck upward.

"It's a human holiday. They're celebrating a different kind of Becoming," Leroy informed them when the boys found him enjoying the night breeze with the radishes.

Hiram liked the way the lights made him feel and it seemed there was a new energy around him. He asked Leroy if he felt it too.

"It's The Becoming you feel, son. It's getting closer for all of us."

"But I'm not ready to Become. I like the

garden and Josh and the peas. Why sometimes I even like those crabby tomatoes!"

"Don't be scared," Josh said. "There's nothing to be worried about."

"Well, I'm still not sure if I like the idea."

"He's afraid of Becoming!" taunted Ham, Ram, Lam and Sam who had overheard them. Hiram ran away and hid behind Ginger.

"What a baby you are," yelled Sylvia, tossing her head.

"I want all of you to leave Hiram alone. Get on home, all of you," Ginger scolded putting her leafy arms around him. "Come on honey, let's go back and talk with Leroy."

"Well Hiram, back so soon?" Leroy teased watching them approach.

"Hiram is still struggling with The Becoming and I thought you could help?"

"Why it would be my pleasure."

"Go ahead, Honey, ask your questions and we'll stay here all night if we need to," Ginger promised.

Blushing, Hiram buried his face in her stalk.

"Nothing to be embarrassed about my boy. The very best of vegetables sometimes need a little extra push. Now, ask away. Don't be shy," Leroy ordered.

Hiram took a deep breath and began,

"What does it feel like? Does it hurt? Won't I be lonesome for all of you? How will I know if I'm ready? Who gets to say if I am ready? Has anyone ever not Become?"

"Mercy, you really do have a lot of questions," Leroy laughed.

"Don't worry. I told you we would answer all your questions tonight and we will," Ginger said.

Leroy began, "I really can't tell you what it feels like, but I know it doesn't hurt, at least I don't think so. And yes, all vegetables Become. No one is left in the garden. In time you'll accept the idea because we all Become with great joy."

"Becoming is our destiny, Hiram," Ginger added, wrapping him in her leaves.

"Becoming is our part in the order of things.

We feed and nourish the humans so they have the energy to think Source thoughts," Leroy said.

Hiram listened, resting in Ginger's leafy arms, but his fear wouldn't go away.

"Maybe I can explain it," Ginger said. "Right now, because you are in the growing process, you're afraid. As you ripen in the safety of the garden, the fear leaves and only your life's purpose remains. I was once very frightened but Leroy and the others taught me to accept and believe in my reason for being."

Hiram wanted to fulfill his purpose and Become. He just hoped it wouldn't hurt too much and he sat talking with his friends long into the night. When yawning, he made his way back to his spot in the garden. He was still afraid, but he trusted Leroy and Ginger and they said he would be happy when it happened.

"Good night, Honey," Ginger said as she settled into her husk bed.

"Sweet dreams Hiram," Leroy added, snug in the warm earth.

"Thank you both," he said, yawning, and was asleep before his head touched the ground.

"Hey Hiram, want to run through the sprinklers with us?" Sylvia asked on a day when the heat in the garden was almost unbearable.

"Yeah, get Josh and join us," her brothers added.

"Okay," Hiram said, and went in search of his friend but when Josh wasn't in his usual place, he went to Leroy.

"Morning Hiram. How's the lad on this very hot summers day?"

"I'm fine sir, but I was wondering if you might know where Josh is. I've looked everywhere."

Leroy looked at Hiram for a long moment and then invited him into the shade. "I'm sorry that Josh didn't have time to tell you son, but the farmer came for him this morning. Josh is to "Become" today and I'm afraid that you won't be seeing him anymore."

Hiram swallowed hard. "Josh is gone sir? He left without saying goodbye? He didn't say anything about being ready to Become? Did he know it?"

"No son, I'm sure he didn't. Josh is your friend and he would never keep a secret from you. The Becoming is very quick for some of us and we have no time to prepare. Other times, we have a long warning, and we've hours to wish each other well before we leave."

Hiram was stunned. The Becoming process had begun, and his friend Josh was the first one called. Hiram mourned for his friend. All day, he sat in the shade beside Leroy, but nothing anyone said comforted him.

Each morning when the farmer came, Hiram stretched as far as he could to see who was being called to Become that day. He grew more confused when his friends went off laughing and waving at him. No one seemed to mind being removed from the garden and their friends.

Even those grumpy tomatoes were happy to go, he thought. He spent the day fretting instead of enjoying the heat of summer.

"Come on Hiram. Quit moping around and come swimming," Sylvia invited.

"Yes," said Ginger. "You should be enjoying yourself with the other young folks instead of wasting these golden days just sitting in your trench."

Hiram tried to join in but he continued to look over his shoulder, dreading the farmer's next visit.

All through that hot month, more and more of his friends left. Hiram began to dread the human's arrival. He would scrunch down low on his vine hoping that the farmer wouldn't see him, and each morning the farmer walked past and took the others. It was a terribly sad time for him because he missed the human's gentle touch.

Next he lost Ham, Lam, Ram, Sam and Sylvia. Hiram began to cry and nothing Ginger or Leroy said could make him stop. He hated The Becoming that tore his friends away and made the garden so lonely.

Well, when he comes for me, I'm going to put up a fight! I'm not going to go laughing. That old farmer is going to know that this little pumpkin doesn't want to go with him, he thought fiercely. He spent the end of August raging and crying and hating the Becoming until he lost some of his wonderful roundness and Ginger had to coax him to drink.

"Please Hiram, you just can't keep carrying on like this."

Hiram turned his face from her and continued to grieve.

He sat in the mud and didn't have the energy to move. What's the use? He pouted as the heat pounded against his face.

He was aware when the farmer opened the gate but he no longer bothered to hide. Anger and fear had consumed him and left him too empty to care. He turned his face away as the farmer began his rounds, but Ginger's voice jarred him back.

"Oh Hiram, it's my turn. I finally get to leave and begin my new journey."

"No, Ginger, don't let him take you!" He screamed as she was placed in the human's basket.

"But Hiram, I want to go honey. I've waited all summer for my turn. Why would I want to stay here?"

"Because you can be with me and Leroy," Hiram cried, hugging her.

"Hiram, you've fought The Becoming until you've made yourself ill. Can't you see my joy and the happiness all the others have shown? I've lived to do this. I wish I could make you understand," Ginger said brushing the leaves back from his face.

"But I'll never see you again. I don't want you to go. Please stay with me and let some other vegetable Become," he sobbed.

"Hiram, do you remember how we used to sit in the garden on those lovely bright nights?" she asked and he nodded. "Do you remember those things the humans call stars?" and he nodded again. "Well, honey, I'll leave my echo there for you. Now, goodbye, love. Take care of yourself."

Just then Leroy appeared and said, "You go

on now, Ginger. Hiram and I will be just fine."

She was gone. He and Leroy waved until they couldn't see her anymore.

"Goodbye Ginger," he called. "I love you and I'll never forget you." Leroy put a leafy arm around him and they sat quietly together for the rest of the day.

• • •

Two mornings later, Leroy left. He had a long warning and he held Hiram all night and talked about his leaving.In the morning when the farmer came, Leroy said to him, "Be brave, my little friend. Your time is coming and then you'll know why we go so joyously. I'm only sad that I must leave you all alone in the garden."

"I love you, Leroy," Hiram whispered and watched and waved as his last friend was carried away in the farmer's arms.

He waited again. All alone, he passed the time by remembering his friends. At night he would think about Ginger and wonder if she was watching over him? Sometimes, he thought he heard Leroy, but he knew it was only his echo.

The golden days passed. Hiram sat abandoned, waiting. The farmer would come each morning and give Him a drink and then hurry away and leave him alone. But Hiram had grown up now and he no longer cried. He simply waited, and waited and...waited.

It grew colder and Hiram used his leaves to cover himself at night. One morning there was ice on the water around his roots. Brrr, he thought, and slept later each day.

The farmer came often. He too, was bundled against the chill. He would spend long hours in the garden as he prepared the seedlings for spring. Hiram listened happily as the farmer made those soothing noises. How good it was to have company again.

He watched as the farmer sorted the baby seeds into packets. They know they're not alone, he thought. They may not know the name yet but they can sense The Source.

At night, He would send his thoughts to the

new life that was quietly waiting to be planted. He didn't know if the small seeds could hear his echo but it kept him from being so lonely.

Then one day it happened. The farmer came and tapped Hiram on the side. He smiled, and with one quick motion, he separated Hiram from his stalk.

Oh no, now it's happening! I'm going to Become. It's finally my turn, he thought and yelled his goodbyes to the resting seeds.

He looked one last time at his garden home as the human carried him away. How small it is, he thought, then turned away from the familiar and prepared for the unknown journey into his Becoming.

The farmer carried him into a strange place and gave him to his wife. She placed him in a tub and bathed him in warm, soapy water. She was very gentle and he wondered could this be The Becoming? If it is, why was I so afraid? This feels wonderful.

She dried him in a fluffy towel. She and the farmer made soft, soothing noises with their mouths as they held him in their hands. Picking up a pencil, she drew on him and he had to fight to keep from laughing because it tickled so.

Then the farmer appeared with a very sharp knife and Hiram knew that it was going to be used on him and he became very, very afraid.

Leroy didn't say anything about a knife. Nobody mentioned being cut. I'm afraid! If this is the Becoming, I don't want it! He almost fainted from fright right there.

Then the most extraordinary thing happened. As the farmer stuck the knife into him, there was no pain. It was the most freeing thing he'd ever known. He was light and happy and the more they carved, the better he felt.

They used a spoon to scoop out his life force but Hiram was glad because he knew he was leaving a strong echo behind. When they cut ears in each side of his head, Hiram heard The Source for the first time.

Next came two eyes and Hiram saw The Source in the humans. He watched as she cut a crooked mouth for him and he smiled his thanks.

I wonder if I have finally Become? Is this it? I wasted all that time being afraid of this? As he sat wondering, the farmer's wife put a candle in his tummy and at dark, she placed him on the front porch. The farmer lit the candle and they stepped back to admire him. Hiram had never been happier. Then they left him and he sat radiating the golden light.

His new ears picked up the wind sighing through the trees. He was overcome with the sound of The Source and he began to Become.

Now that he had eyes, he saw the moon rise and set. He continued to watch as stars peeked through the blackness above and he thought of Ginger. He knew that he was looking at The Source and he Became a little more.

The light in him grew brighter as he felt The Source and he couldn't keep it locked inside and using his crooked mouth, he began to sing a love song to it.

All evening, Hiram waited, softly singing and his Becoming was almost complete. Happily shining his light into the darkness, he heard the farmer's clock chime the hour. The candle in his tummy dimmed, and on the last stroke of midnight, it flickered and died and Hiram was no more.

He had no idea where he was or how he came to be there. It was dark and cold but not uncomfortable. He knew he wasn't alone and feeling snug and cozy, he waited.

Soon light began to creep in. He yearned to touch it and soon the loving light was all around him and he thought he heard a voice call, "Hiram?"

But he wasn't sure, and he waited quietly, wrapped in the light.

Then the voice called from the light again, "Hiram?"

And he answered, "Yes, I'm here!"

The Source said, "Welcome home, Hiram. I've been waiting for you for a long time, and Hiram knew that his waiting was over. He had Become.